DIARY OF A
FRANTIC KID SISTER

DIARY OF A FRANTIC KID SISTER

by Hila Colman

CROWN PUBLISHERS, INC.
NEW YORK

Printed in the United States of America

Library of Congress Catalog Card Number:
72-92388

ISBN: 0-517-502623

Published simultaneously in Canada by General
Publishing Company Limited

First Edition

The text of this book is set in 14 pt. Bodoni Book.

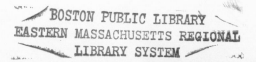

For Sarah Colman

DIARY OF A FRANTIC KID SISTER

September 13

Leave it to me to start my diary on the 13th. I'm the kind who is sure to be called on when I haven't done my homework and goes running for the bus just when it's pulling out. But my bad luck goes deeper than that. People (my mother and Mutsie, my best friend) say I have a fantastic smile and a "zest for life"—they think I am cheerful and happy, but neither of them know I am full of hate and anger. Sometimes I even want to kill people. One person in particular.

This diary is my birthday present from me to me. I promise to tell only the real truth here, at least as well as I can. I will be eleven years old this week, and I already know that everyone lies. My parents lie, my teachers lie, the principal of my school lies. Why do people bother to lie when everyone knows they're lying? Especially her—she lies all the time and thinks she gets away with it. I hate her. And now I told a lie because I can't even say that I hate her. At least not all the time.

She is my sister Didi, whose full name is Deirdre. All you have to do is say her name and then mine—plain Sarah—to know what my parents expected of their firstborn and then of me. But that's only half of it. They went and had our birthdays in the same week. Didi was fifteen yesterday (Tuesday) and my birthday is Saturday. My parents are pretty thoughtful but they didn't figure that sharing your birthday week with an older sister takes away a lot of the fun. It's hard to have something that's entirely yours when there's someone there ahead of you all the time.

I must stop being bugged by Didi. But that's one reason for this diary. I decided that if I write down all my feelings maybe they'll go away. My language teacher says that a lot of writers work out their emotions in their books and autobiographies. I sure hope that happens to me.

I try to see Didi's side of it, but I think she would be happy if I were dead. I can see her taking over my room which she says is bigger than hers. Even when I measured it with a ruler and showed her that hers was bigger she laughed and said that I couldn't measure straight. She'd also take my turquoise ring which she's always had her eye on. She doesn't like to see me enjoy anything.

Like when she came into my room yesterday and picked up my new skinny sweater. She held it up against her and looked at herself in the mirror.

"Forget it," I said. "It won't fit."

"These sweaters fit everyone."

"I'm flatter than you are."

"You sure are," she said, pulling the sweater over her head.

"You'll pull it all out of shape."

"I'm not going to hurt it."

She had the sweater on, and her boobs really stood out. She looked terrific. "I think I'll get one in red," she said. "It'll be fantastic, better than this dead blue."

"You really think this blue is dead?" I asked.

"It's all right for you." She said it kindly.

I really am mixed up about her. Mom says I shouldn't be jealous. That when I'm older I'll do all the things that Didi does, but that's not the point. I don't want to be like Didi, even though she's tall and has a figure like Jane Fonda; I'm small and dark. It isn't jealousy. It's hating her laugh sometimes, and her secrets, and her endless telephone conversations with her friend Ellen—I wish I knew what they talked about so much. And most of all her treating me like a baby. When I want her to be friendly, she turns cold. And then in the middle of hating her, she starts being funny and I feel ashamed of myself.

Got a nice compliment today. My friend Charlotte said I looked like an Indian. I would love to look exotic, like a foreign (or Indian) princess. There's a black girl in our school who wears a turban on her head, and if I wanted to look like anyone it would be like her.

Got to go now. Mom's calling me for dinner. See you later.

I'm terrible for not writing in you every day, and so much has happened that I hope I remember it all. School was pretty good this week. I got an *A* in my social studies paper although Daddy said my handwriting was terrible. He uses a typewriter, and Didi does too, but they make me practice my handwriting. That gets me mad. If I'm going to use a typewriter later what do I need good handwriting for?

They started a new system in our school last year. Everyone's supposed to work on his own —you go to classes, but there's a "resource center" (it's really a big library), where you work on your own project. Some of the kids goof off, which I think is dumb. I'm no big brain but I like to learn things. What's the point of spending so many hours in school if you don't? I told Mr. Harris, my soc. study teacher, I wanted to study anthropology.

He has a beard and wears wild shirts, but I think he's really a square. "That's a big subject," he said.

"So what? I've got all year, haven't I?"

"I wonder if you even know what anthropology means?" He was looking right past me (we were standing in the hall) at the older girls coming out of gym in their leotards. My sister was one of them.

"It's studying about people, isn't it?" He might at least have looked at me while I was talking. "I like to know about different kinds of people. Primitive tribes and stuff like that."

"You'll have to be more specific. Why don't you read some books first? Read Margaret Mead, and pick out what people you want to study. We'll talk about it later." He was halfway down the hall by the time he finished his sentence. Hell. They tell you you can pick any subject you want and then they give you grief when you do. I thought a teacher was supposed to be encouraging. They think more about their silly band and their basketball team around there than about anyone learning anything.

Anyway yesterday was my birthday. It was a nice day. I could see the reservoir in Central Park from my window and the water was all blue and sparkling with the gulls swooping around (they remind me of Cape Cod and I wished I could jump right in). But I'm not allowed to go to the park, which is disgusting, but I go anyway. I wonder what it would be like to be mugged. It's mostly kids and I think I could fight back if there was only one. Or maybe I could talk him out of it. He would ask me to join his gang and I could be the leader and get them to do something good like planting trees or something.

To get back to my birthday. I put a big pink bow on Midnight, my cat. Didi came into my room and said, "That cat looks ridiculous."

"She looks cute. It's for my birthday."

"Oh. Happy birthday." She came over and kissed me. "Take that crazy ribbon off poor Midnight."

"I like it."

"She's your cat." She tried to pick up Midnight, but Midnight doesn't always like to be picked up, and she ran under the bed. "That stupid cat." Didi was furious.

"She's fussy." I couldn't help but laugh. She went out of my room in a huff.

What a way to start off my birthday. I always feel crummy when I have a run-in with Didi, even when I answer her back.

Sometimes when she is late coming home, I imagine she's been kidnapped or has run away.

She disappears and we never see her again. She might be off somewhere living happily but we wouldn't know where and after a while we'd forget all about her. It's dopey because Mom and Dad wouldn't forget, but they'd have me, and I would be a fantastic daughter. I wonder if being an only child is lonesome?

Mom and Dad gave me a record player, which is great. Didi gave me ten dollars for records (which she got from Mom and Dad) and Mom said, "I hope you buy a couple of good records with it." Meaning Brahms or Beethoven. She really wants me to be "musical," like herself and Didi. Which I'm not.

I'm going to buy the wildest, most far-out records I can find. Sometimes I hate music. Mom was a concert pianist, before I was born, and Didi wants to be a singer (fat chance), and they're always at the piano. They scream if I interrupt them, even if it's something important like needing to know a history date, or getting a splinter out of my finger. They say, "Can't you wait until we're finished?" Mom acts like it's her career, not Didi's. She gets so excited when Didi's practicing a new song. Sometimes Mom makes me feel sad.

She gets so sentimental when Didi plays in

the school band, and she talks about her concert days with a quivery look that makes me feel lumpy in my throat.

Then there was the whole thing about my party. Mom had said weeks ago I could have a party on my birthday, so I talked to Mutsie about it, and she thought it was super. We decided to have lunch at my house and to go to a movie. Then Mutsie and I decided who to ask. Everything was planned.

Then along came Didi. "I have the most fantastic idea for my birthday," she said.

"You can't have a big party," Mom said. "You can have some girls over, the way Sarah is doing. . . ."

"I don't want a party. And certainly not what Sarah is doing. Ellen and I thought it would be fantastic if she and Bill and Ronnie and I went out to dinner and to the theatre. We don't have to go to a fancy restaurant—it wouldn't be expensive. Can I?"

Didi threw her arms around Mom in a way that was disgusting.

"It seems to me you're seeing an awful lot of that boy. You're much too young to be going steady with anyone."

Didi laughed the laugh I hate. "Oh, Mom,

11

people don't go steady anymore. Ronnie and I like each other. We're good friends."

"I'll bet. Being mushy all over the place," I said.

"You mind your own business. Can I, Mom?"

"I'll have to discuss it with your father. It seems to me you're a little young for that kind of an evening. I assume you mean just the four of you without a chaperon."

"I don't believe you. You really live in some other world. Perhaps you'd suggest a duenna, some old witch dressed in black who would rap us on the knuckles with her cane if we held hands. Honest to God, Mom, you're out of it."

"I suppose you'll get a new dress too," I mumbled. My movie was looking pretty dull.

"You shut up."

"We'll have to think about it, Didi. Do you want to practice some music with me?"

"Sure, in a minute."

And in five minutes they were playing and singing away as if everything was settled—and you can bet it was. When Didi graduates from high school next year she says she's going to drama school to study voice and acting. She sure doesn't need many lessons in acting; everything she does is an act.

And of course that night it was agreed and she spent about two hours on the phone with Ellen and then with Ronnie. I thought about taking her phone off the hook—that really gets her mad—but she wasn't off the phone long enough to do it.

I was sitting in my room trying to convince myself that going to a movie with a few girl friends was a neat way to celebrate a birthday, when Didi came in.

"What are you doing for your birthday?"

"Hiring Madison Square Garden."

"I hear you're going to the movies. Can't you think of something more original?"

"I haven't got your know-how."

She patted Midnight and then walked out. "Have a good time," she called.

"It's not for a week," I yelled. "I may see you before then."

"Of course, silly."

I can't understand why people make such a fuss about ages. What difference does it make when you were born? Everyone should be equal. It's like discriminating against someone because she is a different color, or has a different religion. It's NOT FAIR.

This is not going to be an ordinary diary. I promise to write in it every day, but then so much happens, I don't. My life is weird. Sometimes it is very boring, but it's also busy.

I've been reading Margaret Mead, and I'm sure glad I didn't live in Samoa—at least when she was there. Little kids there get ordered around by their older sisters *constantly,* and the girls are stuck with the babies while the boys go reef fishing. The girls do all the dirty work around the house, and the older Samoan girls are always telling the younger ones to "Keep still," "Sit still," "Keep your mouths shut." Maybe Didi lived in Samoa in another life.

When I talked to Mr. Harris about it, he said, "An anthropologist has to study cultures objectively. Not pass judgment. Why are you so intense about everything?"

"I'd rather be intense than a cold fish."

"And what do you mean by that?" he asked.

"I mean I'm glad I feel things strongly."

"Perhaps you should learn to use your head more instead of your emotions."

Screw him. I'd like him to teach me something, not analyze me. I wonder if he's using his head when he's watching the girls in their leotards.

"That Mr. Harris is the worst phony," I said to Didi.

"He's cute. I like him."

"That's because he flirts with you."

"Do you think so?" she asked.

"As if you didn't know it. He's a jerk." Didi walked away smiling. I am never going to be boy-crazy the way she is.

Right now, though, I've got another problem. There's this girl Mildred in my class. She's okay, I guess, but she smells. No one likes her and I feel sorry for her, but I haven't tried to make friends with her. I'm afraid my friends will think I'm peculiar if I start going around with her. It makes me feel bad. I think I'd die if nobody liked me. Mutsie and Charlotte are both popular, and being with them makes me feel good.

But I don't have one special friend, the way Didi has Ellen. I never have long telephone conversations the way they have. I don't like Ellen very much, she acts like I don't exist even more than Didi does. When they're together they're always shooing me away like I was spying on them. This is my house too, and when they're in the kitchen I have a right to go in there if I want something. I'm not trying to listen to their dumb conversations.

Just this afternoon Didi said to me, "Do you have to drink your Coke in the kitchen?"

"Why shouldn't I?"

"Because we're here," Ellen said. As if it were her house.

"Tough   ."

"Where'd you pick that up?"

"From you, wise guy," I said. "Mom should hear some of the things you say."

"Let's go into your room," Ellen said, "and close the door." And off they went. Of course I really didn't want to stay in the kitchen by myself, but I did. I don't want to know their secrets, but they could at least be FRIENDLY.

I had intended to tell Didi that I was glad she made the varsity basketball team, but she didn't give me a chance. At school everyone was telling me how wonderful it was and I kept saying, yes, it's fantastic. But now I know it's going to make her even more impossible.

Sometimes I imagine my whole family dead.

Usually it's a car accident. Sometimes it's my parents and I am left with Didi, but I choose not to live with her and go to live with my grandmother. Didi begs me to stay with her, but I say no. She thinks she has to be a mother to me (God forbid), but I put that down, and after a while she discovers that she needs me more than I do her.

The other dream is that Didi is with them when the accident happens. But I don't like that one much because it makes me scared about being all alone. I sometimes wonder if I should ask Mom to send me to a shrink. Some of the kids in my class go but I don't know why, or if it helps them. But Mom would ask why, and I would be afraid to tell her. Thinking about people dying just comes into my head, especially at night if Mom and Dad are out late and I keep listening for them to come home and they don't. Signing off for supper now.

October

Conversation at school. New phys. ed teacher: "Are you Didi Grinnell's sister?"

"Yes, I am." (So what?—not said aloud.)

"She's a fine athlete. Good in basketball and swimming. Do you like sports too?"

"No, I hate sports."

Look of pain passes over teacher's face. "I don't believe you hate *all* sports. There must be something you like?"

"Playing Monopoly. Fishing. My father loves fishing. I wish we had fishing at school."

"You're being fresh . . ." She flips through cards. Finds it. "Sarah."

"I'm not being fresh, Miss Stanley. Really I'm not."

"Well, I hope I can get you to enjoy basketball." She looks me over. "A little exercise would do you good."

God bless Miss Stanley. May she get hit on the head with a basketball.

Still October

Sometimes I can't believe my mother. She acts like a ten-year-old with Didi, the way they laugh and whisper. You'd think a mother would act more dignified. There were secrets going on in our house all week. Even Daddy asked why they were whispering so much. He teased Mom about living her girlhood over again with her daughters. She said, "It's fun to have a teen-age daughter." Wasn't she ever eleven?

My father is tall, with broad shoulders and a moustache, but sometimes he acts like a little mouse. Mom keeps saying she's going to discuss things with him and that he makes the decisions, but I don't believe it. I think she decides. I don't know if I'll ever get married, but if I do, I'll never have secrets in my house. It's disgusting.

Last night Mom brought out some pictures and clippings of her concert tours. She was very beautiful. But it was a peculiar evening. Didi made a big fuss about them, Daddy was very quiet, and Mom was teary-eyed. I think Mom wishes she was still doing it. Margaret Mead says you can be married and have kids and still be an anthropologist. I don't see why Mom can't still give concerts.

I had a real weird experience yesterday. Out of the clear blue Mildred came up to me after math class and said, "You want to come home with me after school?" I was curious and she didn't seem to smell then. Maybe she doesn't smell at all, and I only thought so before because someone said she did.

She lives in a funny little house behind some other houses in a courtyard in Greenwich Village. I thought it was pretty and kind of fun to live in a house in New York (everybody I know lives in apartments), but Mildred said that sometimes the roof leaked and that no one ever fixed anything.

No one was home when we got there and the house was pretty messy. "You hungry?" Mildred asked. I said I was, but all we could find were two bananas, and we had to wash a couple of glasses to split a Coke we found. I had a feeling she wanted to talk, but didn't know how, so we sat around. I was a little sorry I had come and glad no one knew I was there.

Mildred wears braces but I think when she gets them off she may be nice looking. She's got blond hair and light blue eyes.

After a while she did talk. "I don't like people very much," she said. "I like being alone a lot." I'd never thought of anyone *wanting* to be alone, and I didn't know what to say. Then she said, "If you swear not to tell anyone, I'll show you something." She made me put up my right hand and swear I'd keep her secret.

She pulled out a whole bunch of papers from under her mattress and showed me drawings she'd made of a lot of the kids and teachers at school. They were very funny, like cartoons, and I really laughed. "They're great," I said. "Why don't you want anyone to know you can draw so well?"

"They're caricatures. Most people think you're making fun of them. People like flattering pictures."

"Did you ever do one of me?" (She'd probably make me look like a freak.)

"No. I only do people I don't like."

"You sure don't like a lot of people." I was pleased that she didn't have one of me. I wished I had a secret to tell her. But I couldn't tell her that the only person in the world that I positively didn't like (except maybe Mr. Harris, and teachers don't count) was my sister, and that was only part of the time.

Mildred is different from other girls. She really doesn't care about what people think of her. Sometimes in school she disagrees with the teacher and even argues back as if she were a grown-up.

Her mother came home with a big, bearded man. They laughed and talked a lot and were very affectionate with each other. Mildred told me privately that she thought Ricky was her mother's boyfriend. I was dying to ask where her father was, but I didn't. Mildred's mother didn't look like a mother—she wore jeans and her hair was long and wild. Later we all walked over to Washington Square Park, and Ricky and Mildred's mother sat with a bunch of kids who were singing and playing guitars. Mildred sang too, but I didn't because other people kept looking at us.

Ricky bought us all pieces of pizza on the way home and he and Mildred's mother—Mildred calls her by her first name, Judy—anyway, Ricky and Judy kept on singing as we walked and that embarrassed me. Judy asked if I wanted to stay for supper, so I called Mom and she said I could if someone brought me home. Ricky said he would.

Millie (her mother calls her Millie so I did too) and I went into her room and she told me that she didn't have a father. I said she had to have one to be born, and she said she knew that but that her father "wasn't around." Then she asked if I could keep another secret. "I've never told this to anyone in my life," she said. "If you tell anyone I'll kill you."

"I think my father is on drugs," she said. Then she turned away and I thought maybe she was crying.

"But you don't know, do you? Why do you think so?"

"I just know." Then she looked scared. "Do you think that will make me crazy? I read that people on drugs can have crazy kids."

"But you're not crazy. You're smart. You can draw. You're not crazy at all."

She looked a little relieved, but I felt scared. It must be awful not to have a father and to worry about being crazy. Like some of the people you see on the street talking to themselves. I always cross to the other side when I see them.

We went into the kitchen and Judy and Ricky were drinking wine but there was no sign of anyone making supper. I was getting hungry.

Then Judy said, "You kids hungry?"

"Yes," replied Millie. "What's there to eat?"

"Not much," Judy said. She opened the refrigerator. "I guess I forgot to market." No one seemed worried.

"I can make an omelet," Millie offered.

"If we had eggs," Judy laughed.

"We can buy eggs," Ricky said.

"Sarah and I'll go to the store," Millie said. She seemed more grown up than her mother. Ricky gave her some money and we left. It was fun. We bought eggs and scallions, and some salad and a big loaf of French bread and some cheese. Millie made a terrific scallion and cheese omelet and we ate it with big chunks of bread. It was better than meat and vegetables and potatoes. We even had a little glass of wine.

After supper Ricky said he would take me home, and Millie and Judy said they'd ride with us. Ricky had a funny jeep, and Judy sat in front with him and Millie and I were in back. When we got to my house, Ricky insisted that he walk me to the door.

I had the funniest feeling when I came home. I felt that for the first time in my life I'd had an experience that was my own and I was not going to tell anyone in my family about it. After the bare rooms at Millie's, our apartment looked comfortable, but I wondered if people really needed so many chairs and tables and lamps and drapes and stuff. Mom hates to vacuum, and maybe she wouldn't have to if she didn't have so much junk.

"Did you have a nice time?" Mom asked.

"Very good."

"You missed some super roast beef," Didi said.

"I don't care."

"Where were you, anyway?" Didi stopped halfway out the room.

"At Millie's."

"At Millie's? That freak! You shouldn't be allowed down there!" Didi put down the dictionary she was carrying. (Why didn't she just go out of the room!)

Dad put down his newspaper. "Why shouldn't she be allowed there, Didi?"

"It's none of her business," I yelled. "She's never been there, she doesn't know." I could have killed her.

"I wouldn't go there on a bet. I know plenty."

"Will you please tell me what this is all about?" asked Dad.

"Everyone at school knows about Mildred

Shimko. Her father's a drug addict and her mother's a Village bum. Millie's probably on drugs herself. She's mixed-up and nobody likes her."

"That's a dirty lie. Millie's smart and her mother's very nice. You don't know anything." I was so mad I was afraid I was going to cry.

"Do you know these things for a fact, Didi, or are they just rumors?" asked Dad in his quiet, let-me-do-the-talking voice.

"It's common knowledge," said Didi. "You can ask anyone at school."

"I don't think you'd better go there until we find out if what Didi says is true," Mom said.

"You're all disgusting. I don't care about Millie's parents, and I don't care if nobody else likes her. I do."

I ran into my room and banged the door shut. But that wasn't good because Mom or Didi could walk in. I went into the bathroom and locked the door. There I could be by myself.

The awful thing was that I wasn't sure I liked Millie that much. Her house was kind of odd, and I didn't really dig her, but they were pushing me. Why couldn't Didi mind her own business? I cried and cried and felt awful.

26

Later, when I heard Didi go out of her room, I sneaked in and took her phone off the hook.

November

School gets so boring. I like to read and write stories, but math, and that dumb phys. ed. I wish I'd break my leg and not have to go to gym. Connie, a girl in my class, broke her ankle and she says that's the only good part of it. I can't decide what tribe I want to study for my project. "You'd better make up your mind," said Mr. H.

"Every time I read another book I get excited about a new place."

"Maybe you'd better stop reading."

"That's funny advice, Mr. Harris. I thought that was what the resource center was for."

"You know what I mean. Stop just reading and get to work."

"If I said reading was work, would that be okay?"

"Cut it out, Sarah. Pick out your project and give me an outline of what you want to do."

"I'd really like to go to Africa. I was thinking maybe I should study something in archaeology instead of anthropology."

"I'm thinking I'd better assign you to study halls. I don't know if you're mature enough to work on your own."

That big jerk. I've read more books than anyone else in my class. Just because I enjoy it, he thinks I'm not working.

The big secret at home finally came out. Mom and Didi were planning a Hallowe'en party for Didi and they didn't want Dad to know, so they didn't tell me. As if I would have told. Sometimes I think those two don't believe that I'm part of this family. Now that Didi goes out with boys (one boy, Ronnie), she always has secrets with Mom. You'd think she'd want to talk to her sister sometimes instead of her mother.

Mom says it's fun having a teen-age daughter, but she gets sad sometimes. It must be terrible to grow old. The other day when I came home from school Mom was in her room, and I think she was crying. She pretended she wasn't so I didn't say anything, but it made me feel bad.

Anyway, Didi had this party, and of course they had to tell Dad. The secret was that it was on the night Mom and Dad were going to be out and they were afraid if he knew in advance he would have said no. He should have, too. I bet they smoked pot, although Didi swears they didn't. But why did she insist that I stay with Grandma? The more I think of it the madder I get. I wonder if they kissed, too? Sometimes Didi stands naked in front of her mirror admiring herself. I wonder if she ever lets Ronnie see her naked. She probably does. She loves to wear clothes that show off her breasts—you'd think no one else in the world had them the way she goes around sticking them out.

Grandma is the only one in my family who treats me like a person instead of some backward freak. I had a good time with Grandma. We watched the news (she's very political and knows a lot); she had a cocktail and gave me a sip. I like the pickled onion at the bottom of the glass the best. Then we had a great time cooking little pieces of meat in her fondue dish. We thought of going to a movie but we couldn't find anything in the neighborhood we wanted to see so we stayed home.

I wanted to tell her about Millie, but I didn't. I can keep a secret. I did ask her why I had trouble making up my mind about things—like my anthropology project—and why I felt dopey about making friends with Millie when the other girls didn't like her.

She said it was hard to think independently. "But it's the most important thing to learn. At least you're trying and that's half the battle." (I must remember that.)

She said a lot of other things—I hope I can remember them all. "Don't be afraid to be different. Your parents may seem conventional to you now, but they weren't always that way."

"Maybe I was adopted."

Grandma laughed. "I was in the hospital when you were born, and believe me you were their baby."

I like to hear about my parents when they were young. "Your mother was a concert pianist," Grandma said, "and that took a lot of hard work. She had a lot of ideas for the future. Your father wanted to be a painter, but he couldn't make a living at it so he became a textile designer. Before you kids were born, they were both struggling against a conventional life."

"They sure aren't now," I said. "Our house is stuffed with furniture and they fuss about food and Dad has a fit if Mom forgets to buy his cigars. Everything has to be just so. In Millie's house they eat when they feel like it and there's nothing there except what they absolutely need. It's neat."

"I think your mother would like yours and Didi's life to be different from hers. She wants Didi to have a career and I suspect she hopes Didi doesn't give it up even when she gets married."

"What about me? Doesn't she want me to have a career?"

"You're a little young yet. Besides, you don't know yet what you want to do, and Didi does."

"I know. That's my trouble."

"It's not a trouble. You have plenty of time."

"I wish they thought so at school. Mr. Harris keeps pushing me."

"I know. It's ridiculous. Nowadays everyone has to be a specialist, even in kindergarten." (I wish Grandma was my teacher.)

I wish Mom and Dad had stayed unconventional. I'd love to live in a loft and have Dad stay home and paint and Mom play in concerts. We don't need a big apartment and a cleaning lady to come in and take care of it. The only thing I'd hate to give up is our house in Truro, but maybe if Dad were an artist we could live there all the time. I'd love that.

November

I'm sick. My nose is stuffed up and I have a sore throat. Even ice cream tastes terrible. Didi brought me a pint of butter pecan (my favorite), and I couldn't even eat it. She can be nice sometimes. She sat on my bed and talked to me about Ellen and Bill—they had a big fight and she thinks they might split up. She said she'd die if she and Ronnie broke up. I wonder if I'll ever have a boyfriend. I don't think I'd ever get moony the way Didi does. Charlotte told me that Howard Dirkson likes me. She thought I'd say he was a drip, but I didn't. I think he's good looking, but I wouldn't tell that to anyone, not even Mutsie.

Mutsie brought me my homework but Mom wouldn't let her into my room because she might catch what I've got. She stood in the door but we couldn't talk about anything because Mom was standing there too. Mr. H. sent me some books on anthropology but they're boring. He's such a drip. I didn't want to do anything except sleep.

Still November

I was home for a whole week before Mom let me go back to school. Because I was absent everyone made a fuss when I came back. It only lasted about five minutes and then things went back to normal.

I don't think I want to do either anthropology or archaeology for my project. I can't talk to Mr. H., but I did talk to Mrs. L., my language teacher. I told her I really wanted to write something. I must like to write because I like writing in this so much. She listens and I don't feel she's thinking of something else while I'm talking to her. I wish I could get rid of Mr. H. and switch to her.

Millie's acting strange. Very quiet, even more than usual. She says her mother may be going away to make a picture—her mother's a film editor—before Christmas, and she's going to have to live with some people she doesn't like. I had a feeling she wanted me to ask her to come and stay with us, but I didn't say anything. It might be awful.

The day after Thanksgiving

Yesterday was the worst day in my life. I was so lonely. And I usually love Thanksgiving. Didi and I always help Mom set the table, and it looks so pretty with Mom's good Italian table-cloth and her good silver and little dishes for nuts, and the place cards I make. My aunt and uncle come from Harrison and then there's my Cousin Lily, and Grandma. Sometimes Dad invites someone from the studio where he works. Mom got up early to put the turkey in the oven and the house smelled so good with the pies and biscuits baking and the super sweet-potato thing that Mom makes.

But this year it was different because Didi went away for the day. It was like breaking a tradition that I thought would always go on.

"People have to grow up," Mom said. It scared me. Not that I didn't think Didi had a right to go up to New Haven with Ronnie and his father for the Yale-Harvard game. I thought Dad was pretty mean to give her a hard time about going. But I had this awful, sinking feeling that everyone I knew—Didi, Mutsie, and Charlotte, were all going to have exciting lives, and I was going to be stuck. I couldn't think of one single thing to look forward to, except maybe Christmas. But that will probably be different now too.

I called Millie in the afternoon because I thought maybe she was feeling lonely, too, but she wasn't—her mother and Ricky had a whole bunch of people there and she was having a great time. That made me feel even more lonesome. I left the grown-ups and sat in my room, pretending to be reading, but I couldn't even do that.

December

Snow. Hooray. Maybe I can ride my sled in Central Park after school. Got to go now.

Much later. Scene: Older sister in room, door halfway open. Younger sister crosses hall to borrow Scotch tape from older sister. Hears telephone conversation. Older sister to friend Ellen: "You're lucky being an only child. Wish I were. That sister of mine is always noseying around. She's the world's worst copy cat . . . she seems to forget she's five years younger than I am . . ."

Dirty lie. Only four years. I took her Scotch tape and the pen I'd lent her a week ago. Accidentally on purpose turned her radio on loud so she couldn't hear Ellen on the phone.

Still December

The snow was still good today and I was able to go sliding. Had a super day. Central Park was all white with little icicles on the trees. Someone was really smart to put the park right in the middle of the city. All the tall buildings around it look like castles (some of them, anyway) and from the distance New York looks clean and pretty.

Mutsie, Charlotte, and I took our sleds out

to the hill in the park and everyone was there. Howard kept looking at me, I could tell. Everyone calls him Howie, but I like Howard better.

"Do you want to go down with me?" he asked.

"Sure."

He got on his stomach and I got on top of him, and off we went. It was fun. He can make his sled go faster and longer, way down around the curve, and at the end we both rolled into the snow. He didn't throw snow on me either. Neither one of us said a word pulling the sled back up the hill but it was nice. All I could think of was corny things to say like how beautiful it was, but I had the sense not to.

I do hope I can be a mysterious woman when I get older. Sometimes I wish I lived in one of those countries where women wear veils over their faces and just their eyes show, but I suppose that gets to be a nuisance when you want to eat or blow your nose.

Howard and I went on his sled again. Sliding must be something like flying—you get a funny feeling in your stomach, and then you feel the wind in your face and everything goes whizzing by. I love it.

He had to go home after a while and I went

back to Mutsie and Charlotte. They teased me but I didn't care. Then a funny thing happened. My red wool scarf that had been tied around my neck was gone. I started looking for it, and Mutsie and Charlotte started giggling.

"We know where it is," Mutsie said.

"Give it to me. I got it last Christmas."

"We haven't got it," Charlotte said.

"Look, I've got to go home."

"Howie has it," Mutsie said.

I didn't believe her. "Why would he have it?"

"You dropped it in the snow and he picked it up and put it in his pocket. We saw him."

"That's dumb. Why would he want my scarf?"

"Because he likes you, stupid. He'll use it as an excuse to go to your house."

"You're crazy."

"Sarah has a boyfriend, Sarah has a boyfriend," they chanted.

"You're obnoxious," I yelled.

I wish I had someone to talk to about boys. Someone who knows more about them than Mutsie or Charlotte or me. What does it mean if a boy "likes" you? It gave me a funny feeling, as if I was supposed to do something about it but I didn't know what.

If Didi were different I could talk to her. Maybe I could talk to Grandma, but I wonder if she knows how things are done now.

Later

It's late and I'm supposed to turn out my light but I'm so angry. I don't know what to do.

When I came home from the park Mom and Didi were at the piano.

"Did you have a good time?" Mom asked.

"Super. It was great."

"Were you sleigh riding?" asked Didi, knowing full well that I was from the way I was dressed.

"No, I was swimming."

"You're impossible. No wonder you don't get along well in school."

"Who says I don't get along well?"

"You wouldn't go around with Millie if you had other friends."

"That's a lie. I have plenty of friends."

"I don't think she should go into the park alone," she said to Mom.

"I wasn't alone. Everyone was there. You mind your own business."

"I wouldn't want to see you mugged," said Didi.

"Didi, don't talk like that." Mom was horrified. "On an afternoon like this, when a lot of kids are out sleigh riding it should be all right. Just be sure to leave well before dark, Sarah."

"Well, I hope I won't have to say I told you so," said Didi.

"You'd probably be glad," I muttered. I wanted to hit her. I never can get back at her when she pulls off that big-sister crap of hers. I don't need her to protect me. Being eleven is the most nothing age.

Still December

I'm really worried about Millie. She looks awful, as if she never goes to sleep. I don't know what to do. I think I'll ask Mom if I can invite her to spend Christmas with us.

I couldn't ask Mom anything because she and
Dad had a big fight. I get nervous when they
have fights. I'd die if they ever got divorced. I
wonder who I'd live with? Mom says that it's
healthier to fight than to keep everything inside.
She says that when she and Daddy disagree it
doesn't mean that they stop loving each other.
"It's normal for people to disagree," she says,
"but you shouldn't sulk or hold a grudge." But
when I fight with Didi I burn about it for days.

Anyway, Mom said at dinner that she wanted
to get a job. You should have seen Dad's face.
As if she said she was going to Africa. "You
have a perfectly good job here in this house,"
he said. "Bringing up two girls and taking care
of the house and of me."

Mom made a face. "That's not what I mean.
I mean something for myself. The girls are growing up. I thought I could do something with my
music."

Dad was horrified. "You can't go back to
playing concerts—practicing every day, going
on the road. That's out."

She stared. "It wouldn't be so terrible. But I

wasn't thinking of that. I'm probably too old to start all over again in that direction. But I could give lessons. I think I'd like that. I like working with young people."

Dad looked disgusted. "That's for a spinster schoolteacher. I don't want my wife giving piano lessons. We don't need the money—it would be demeaning."

"Demeaning to who?" Mom was furious. "You don't think it's demeaning to me, a concert pianist, to be a household drudge all these years? To have to ask you for every cent I want to spend?"

I was so excited I wanted to cheer. Dad looked scared. "You've been reading all that women's lib junk. You were perfectly content until all that stuff started coming into the house."

"That's what you think. You don't even think I'm capable of doing my own thinking! I'm bringing up two girls—what kind of an example am I setting for them? I'm wasting my life and when the girls are grown up and out of the house what am I supposed to do? Play bridge every afternoon or start drinking because I'm bored . . . don't you dare tell me what to do, don't you dare . . . " She started sniffing and then got up and left the table and we all knew she was crying.

None of us said a word. Dad sat there making believe he was eating and looking sullen. Finally he got up from the table and swore. "I hope you girls don't get crazy ideas," he muttered. He went into the living room and started reading the newspaper but I doubt that he read anything.

After a while Mom came back and started clearing the table with Didi and me helping her. "I'm sorry, kids," she said. "I didn't mean to make a scene."

"I'm not going to let anyone interfere with my career," Didi said.

"I hope not," Mom said.

"Me neither," I said.

"You'll probably get married and have a million kids," Didi said.

"What do you know? You don't know a damn thing about me."

"Now, girls, don't you two fight. We've had enough for one night."

I felt all churned up inside, but writing it down has made me feel better. I think I have really made up my mind. I do want to be a writer. I've got to get up my courage and talk to Mrs. L. about it. Maybe I can switch from Mr. H. to her. I want to write a play. I think writing a play is more important than singing or acting in one. The actress only says words that someone else wrote first.

Christmas Eve

I like Christmas Eve best of all—almost better than Christmas, I think. It snowed again, which made it perfect. I can look out of my window at the park. It's all white and the lights around the city twinkle. It makes me feel that the world is a nice place. It is hard to believe that people are starving (I wonder what it feels like to have *nothing* to eat?) and that people are fighting and killing each other. I hope there are no more wars when I grow up.

Our house looks beautiful. Didi and I decorated the Christmas tree; it's in front of the window in the living room and it looks super. Mom bought some beautiful new ornaments and the whole tree is silvery. We turned out the lights after supper and had only the tree lights on. Mom played carols and Mom and Dad and Didi and Grandma and I sang them. We always have a special Christmas Eve dinner. Tonight we had real Russian caviar on little crackers, and Didi and I each had a glass of champagne. Then we had roast duck and orange, and a spinach casserole and lemon meringue pie. Mom is a very good cook, and even though she is a concert pianist, or was, I think she likes to cook too.

I don't know what happened at the end of Mom and Dad's fight, but she hasn't said anything more about giving piano lessons. I hope she doesn't give up, and I'm going to tell her not to one of these days. Didi said I should mind my own business, but I don't know why I can't tell my own mother something that's for her own good.

Still December

I guess I'm truly cuckoo. First I can't wait for Christmas vacation, and now in the middle of it I'm waiting to go back to school. Nuts.

Christmas day was super. I got books and records, and some money, and a new sweater, and a pair of white boots. Didi got a terrific new ski outfit, so her old one got handed down to me (natch). It's pretty new looking but it doesn't fit me too well yet. Mom says I'll grow into it. I'd rather grow into a new one.

Still vacation

Something nice happened today. The doorbell rang and who should be there but Howard. He said, "I was walking by and remembered I had your scarf in my pocket so I thought I'd drop it by." Then he asked me if I wanted to go out for a walk. Mom was out but Maggie, our cleaning lady, was there so I told her I was going out, and we went.

We walked all the way down to 42nd Street, and talked about everything. He told me about his older brother who is in California in college and didn't have the money to come home for Christmas. Howard sounded sorry, but proud of

46

his brother and made me feel ashamed of the way I feel about Didi. We talked about the kids in our class and we agreed about almost everyone. I didn't ask him if he liked Millie. He feels the same way about Mr. H. that I do. By the time we got downtown we were cold and Howard suggested that we stop and have some hot chocolate. We had a good time.

Tonight I didn't care about watching Didi get dressed up to go out to a movie with Ronnie.

December

Hooray! We're going skiing for New Year's weekend. I'm so excited!

Mutsie asked if I like Howard. "Sure I do," I told her. Then she started in again about my having a "boyfriend." She's six months older than I am, and she's silly when it comes to boys. She doesn't understand that Howard is a friend, not a "boyfriend." I think Mutsie pretends to be more grown up than she is. I wish she didn't.

New Year!!!

I look at the last entry in this diary and I want to SCREAM. I honestly thought that New Year's weekend was going to be terrific, but it was a disaster. Except for one thing.

This is what happened: We'd been talking about the weekend constantly, planning to go up to Vermont, probably Stowe, and it was going to be fantastic. Dad got reservations in a cottage we were going to have all to ourselves (but near the main house), and I couldn't wait. Then all of a sudden at dinner (everything in our house happens at the dinner table), Didi said, "Can I stay home New Year's weekend?"

"Of course not," Mom said. "I wouldn't dream of leaving you here alone."

Didi's mouth started getting set, but twitchy too. "I wouldn't be alone. Ellen could stay with me. No one my age has to spend New Year's Eve with their parents. I'm not a baby." The creep looked at me as if I were still in diapers!

"If you're thinking of a New Year's Eve party here, forget it," Dad said.

"No, I won't forget it. I'm sick and tired of being treated like Sarah. I'm five years older and I don't want to do the same things she does. It's ridiculous."

"Four years older," I snapped.

"You cannot have a New Year's Eve party with all of us away. That's out." Mom sounded firm, but then she often does until Didi makes her change her mind.

"It would only be four couples, eight kids. Ellen and Bill, Ronnie and me, and Connie and Nick and Sue and Hugh. You know all of them . . . We would just sit around and play records and dance . . ."

"I thought Ellen and Bill were splitting up," I said.

Didi gave me a dirty look. "They're not. Not now anyway." I wondered why she looked so tense. As if her life depended on her New Year's Eve party. Something was going on.

"You should have spoken up before and maybe we wouldn't have planned it." Mom's voice trailed off.

"Please. It's important to me."

"It's too late. You had no business planning anything like that. You're coming with us, period." Dad was really firm.

"What's so great about a New Year's Eve party?" I asked.

"You wouldn't understand." She looked as if she was either going to cry or kill someone and got up and left the table.

Later

I wish I knew what was going on. I hate all this mystery and secrets. Didi's been in her room crying and Mom and Dad have been having private conversations. No one has asked me what I want to do for New Year's Eve. We used to have such good times going on picnics and skiing weekends, and swimming at Truro. And now Didi is ruining everything. It's stinky. I wish she didn't have a boyfriend. She never even plays Monopoly with me anymore. She says she "doesn't have time"—but she sure has time to talk on the phone.

Finally I spoke up. "Are we going away skiing or not? I wish someone would tell me what we're going to do."

"Yes, we're going skiing," Mom said.

"Didi too?"

"No. She's going to stay home and have her party."

I was furious. "If she stays home, I want to too. There won't be any kids up there, and I wouldn't know them anyway. I won't have any fun going away with you two," I said. "Why can't I be with my friends New Year's Eve?"

"I'm not going to have a party with her around," Didi shouted.

"I can stay with Grandma."

"No you can't. Grandma's staying here with Didi," Dad said.

That was the last straw. "Then why can't I? I live here."

"I'm not going to have that kid hanging around all weekend. Grandma's busy all day Saturday, she's only coming to sleep here Saturday night. I'm not playing nursemaid."

"I don't need a nurse, you creep." I picked up a dumb doll Ronnie had given Didi (it was some stupid private joke of theirs) and threw it. I really thought it would land on her bed, but it hit the floor and smashed into pieces.

"You creep! Get out of my room, just get out!" Didi was white. Mom and Dad kind of pushed me out of the room, and they went out too. Didi slammed the door, and I went into my room and slammed my door. I don't know what Mom and Dad did, but Mom looked awful.

I'm scared. Something's happening. Mom is very touchy, Dad sometimes looks grim. I'm not so sure Mom still thinks having a teen-age daughter is so much fun. Having a teen-age sister STINKS. I was a little sorry I broke her doll. "If she's so grown up, what does she need a doll for?" I asked Mom.

"I guess because Ronnie gave it to her." Mom sighed.

"She wouldn't even give me a chance to say I was sorry. She just said she didn't want to speak to me."

"Leave her alone. She'll get over it," Mom said.

You can bet I'll leave her alone.

New Year's weekend was TERRIBLE, except for one tiny part of it. The drive up was long and boring. Mom kept telling me what a good time I was going to have, which convinced me that she knew better. Her attempts at being cheerful fell flat—she was worried about leaving Didi home. The only kids up there kept to themselves, and there was one dopey girl about a year older than me who could hardly ski at all.

By Sunday afternoon I was so bored I could scream. My parents were going skiing and then to a cocktail party at the main house. They wanted me to go with them, but I didn't feel like it. I told them I was going to stay in the cottage and read. They told me to be sure to come up later for the party. What was I going to do at a grown-up cocktail party?

I read for a while and then decided to go for a walk. It was a nice day, which depressed me. I could have been home sled riding with my friends in Central Park instead of being stuck in Vermont with nobody. It was cold and crisp but the sun was warm. I walked up a little path in the woods. There were a lot of pine trees with snow on them.

It was absolutely quiet. I walked and walked, not knowing where I would come out. It was fantastic. I felt very solemn, something like being in church. I'm not a religious person, and I don't really know if there is a God. Howard believes in nature; he says there is a force stronger than man that created the Universe. Anyway, suddenly I wasn't afraid. I went 'way deep into the woods, and I felt as if I could walk forever. *I liked being alone.* I couldn't believe it. I was suddenly discovering something fantastic—that I never had to be afraid just because I was alone. Like I'd always be with me, if you know what I mean. I'd always have my own thoughts. I felt like I had suddenly found a friend in myself. That sounds cuckoo, but it's the way I felt.

When I came back my mother and father were panicking. They'd come back to the cottage to look for me and I wasn't there. I don't know where they thought I could have gone, except for a walk. Parents are sometimes pretty cuckoo.

January

Vacation's over, and I'm not sorry. I got up my nerve and told Mrs. L. I wanted to switch from social science (Mr. H.) to her, and that I wanted to write a play. "Do you like the theatre?" she asked me.

"I haven't been to many plays. But I like to write dialogue. I like it better than writing about things."

"I'm all for your trying. Why not? But I suggest you read some plays first. Do you know what you want to write about?"

I could have lied to her and said yes, but I didn't.

"No, I don't. Maybe it will be about a family."

She gave me some plays to read. I'm excited about it. I like Mrs. L.

January

I invited Millie up to spend the day with me. Her mother hasn't gone away yet, but she's going soon. I don't think she liked our house too much—too many things in it. We went for a walk and Millie said that Central Park West was dull and that the Village was more fun. She's right. We talked a lot and she said that her mother was wacky but she didn't mind because she didn't have to do things like being on time for meals and going to bed at a certain hour. But then I thought that she did a lot of other things that I didn't have to do, like shopping and cooking and washing up dishes by herself.

February

I'm glad January is over. It was awful. Not that February will be much better, but here's hoping. I always keep thinking that something is going to happen that will change everything. Like Didi disappearing, or going back to how she used to be (not a TEEN-AGER), or something happening to my parents so that I could go and live with Grandma. Maybe I'm sick because I think such awful things. But I wish something exciting would happen. Sometimes I dream I save someone from a fire, or stop a burglar in our apartment. I don't want to be an ordinary person with an ordinary life.

February 14

I got a Valentine card. I really got two. Grandma always sends me one, but I got another one that wasn't signed. Mutsie said Howard probably sent it, but I bet she did just to be funny. I wish she and Charlotte would stop teasing me about his being my "boyfriend."

I don't know *anything* about boys. Everyone talks about sex but no one actually tells you anything. If everyone in the world has intercourse and everyone gets born the same way, I don't understand why it is kept such a secret. It's wild. My mother says she'll tell me anything I want to know about sex, but she gets a funny look when she even mentions the subject, so I know she doesn't want to talk about it. I can't imagine being naked in front of a boy, much less intercourse.

February

It snowed all day and all night and it's still coming down. The whole city is white, and it is so beautiful. I went out for a walk in the snow. There were lots of kids in the park with their nurses or mothers. My mother used to take me to the park when I was little, and I wonder if I looked like that and if she loved me then. I didn't want to think about Mom or Didi so I didn't think about anything except watching the snow fall and the icicles on the trees and the kids playing. There were two little girls dressed alike, although one was older than the other, and I knew they were sisters. They were laughing and rolling in the snow. I think Didi and I used to be that way. We have pictures of when we were little playing together on the beach and in the park. It was good then—before she started growing up and left me behind.

I walked and walked and kept my mind empty of everything except what I was seeing. I think that's a good thing to do for someone who's going to be a playwright. Mrs. L. says a writer has to keep his mind open. Like a pot with the lid off so that you can absorb all kinds of weather, people around you, strangers, sights, sounds, and smells. A writer has to be something like a strainer: to let in everything, including the gook, and then sort it out.

Still February

Something is going on with Didi. After she talked to Ronnie on the phone last night, she closed her door and I'm sure she was crying. And she's so touchy. Mom said at dinner, "You look tired, Didi. I think you ought to stay home this weekend."

Didi flew off the handle. "Stop telling me I look tired. You say that because you don't want me to see Ronnie. You just want me to stay home and play the piano with you all the time."

"That's not fair. One has nothing to do with the other. I think you need more rest." Mom was really hurt.

"I get plenty of rest. Just leave me alone."

I have a mean streak in me. I get a perverse pleasure when Mom and Didi fight.

But today was scary. Mom and I came home from shopping and when we got off the elevator on our floor we smelled gas. Mom panicked. "There's a leak," she said. "Maybe there'll be an explosion."

I could see Didi lying on the kitchen floor with the oven turned on. It was awful. There was a scrawled note on the kitchen table saying that she couldn't go on living. I saw myself on the floor trying to give her artificial respiration. ELEVEN YEAR OLD SAVES SISTER . . .

In the meantime Mom had rushed us downstairs and the superintendent said he would go into our apartment. He was pretty casual and said the pilot light on the stove had probably gone out. Mother insisted we wait downstairs until he found out.

"Someone didn't turn one of your burners all the way off. I opened the window. It's okay now," he said when he came back down.

"It must have been Didi," I said. "She came home from school before she went for her music lesson."

"I'm worried about Didi," Mom said. I waited for her to tell me more, but she didn't.

I really expected Didi to catch hell when she got home. I mean she could have killed all of us if the stove had exploded or the gas caught fire. But Mom was calm and spoke to her quietly. Sometimes I think Mom's afraid of Didi's temper—she's always handling her with kid gloves. "Teen-agers are touchy," I heard her say to Maggie. It gets me mad.

When Dad came home I told him what had happened. And then Didi got mad at me. "Why don't you mind your own business? I'm quite capable of telling him what I did myself. You didn't have to blurt it out the minute he walked in the door."

"I can tell him anything I please. Don't you

tell me what to tell my own father, or when. You dictator."

"All right, cool it, girls." Dad was annoyed.

I went into my room and put my record player on real loud, which annoys the hell out of her. She says she can't think, but it really bothers her on the telephone.

Still nasty February

Mom and Didi went to a concert and I stayed home with Dad. After I finished my homework, I watched a TV show in the dining room while he was in the living room reading. The house was quiet and it gave me a nice feeling to know that Dad and I were alone in the house.

The show was weird. It was about two homosexuals. Dad came in before the show was over and watched the end of it with me. He asked me why I had picked that show to watch. "I didn't know what it was about," I told him. "I just happened to turn on that station."

He was frowning. "Do you know what a homosexual is?"

"I think so. I'm not absolutely sure."

"They're different sexually, that's all." He was still frowning. "I don't suppose it hurts you to see something like that . . . I'm not sure . . ." He seemed to be talking to himself.

"It doesn't bother me." Then I looked up at him. "Do you think I'm normal?"

He didn't laugh at me. "I don't think you have to worry about that."

"I sometimes have pretty morbid thoughts."

"Everyone does. You think pleasant things too, don't you?"

"Sometimes." I wanted to ask him if it was all right to hate Didi, but when I thought about saying it out loud I knew it wasn't true. I don't really hate her—she just gets me mad sometimes.

It was nice being with Dad. He often acts removed when everyone's home, as if he's not paying attention. But then he surprises you by saying something and you know he hasn't missed a thing. I think I love Dad best of all, and Grandma second. It makes me feel disloyal to Mom, but she has Didi.

March

I'm sick of winter. I love going barefoot and wearing shorts and walking on the beach. Now it's all slushy out and dull, and while spring is supposed to be only a few weeks away, there's no sign of it yet.

I worry about Mom and Dad growing old. Millie said, "What would you do if your parents were killed in an automobile accident?" It was creepy, as if she could read my thoughts. I don't want to die. Maybe there will be some awful disaster and we'll all die together. I like to think about reincarnation when I get scary thoughts. I'd like to come back and be someone different, the only trouble is I don't know if I would know who I had been before. I wonder if I've had any different lives before.

Later in March

I had a nice afternoon with Grandma. She took me to the day-care center where she works a few days a week. The kids were really cute. I was sorry I didn't have Midnight with me to show them. They were shy at first, but I played games with them, and they all wanted to wear my turquoise ring. Grandma says it breaks her heart to see the homes they go back to. I think things should be evened up more. I read in the paper about some woman who bought a diamond for $450,000. What will she do with it? It's disgusting.

Still March

Millie and I are getting to be good friends. She came uptown Saturday and we went for a walk in the park. It was nice out, it smelled almost like spring. Millie looked kind of crazy in big plaid slacks and an old, dirty blue denim jacket missing most of its buttons.

Some boys were having a ball game in the park and Millie stood and watched them so intently I asked her what she was doing. She was embarrassed and said, "Nothing." But later she said, "I was trying to memorize what they looked like so I can draw them later. I'd like to draw them running that way." I realized that when she looked that way she wasn't squinting, but concentrating, and I thought that was okay.

We went to the Metropolitan Museum of Art, and she was fantastic. She knew where everything was. She said, "Let's look at the French Impressionists," or "Let's look at the religious paintings, or the Corots and the Rembrandts and Goyas." She pulled me around from room to room, but I got to one case out in a hall where I could have stayed for hours. In it was a group of miniature Degas pieces of sculpture of ballet figures and horses. Each one was perfect. He made being a dancer the most fantastic thing in the world. I wonder if a writer can make anyone feel that way.

When Millie came to take me away I felt heavy and dumpy. Out in the street I revived a little, and Millie said she wanted to stop at Lamston's to get a few things. I didn't feel at all like going to the dime store, but I went anyway. We wandered from counter to counter, losing each other every once in a while the store was so jammed. Finally Millie said, "Let's go."

"Did you get what you want?" I asked her.

"Sure, come on."

"Where is it?" She wasn't carrying any bag.

"Shut up. Let's get out of here." She walked quickly for about a block without saying anything, dragging me along with her. "What'd you buy?"

"I didn't *buy* anything, you idiot." She pulled out of her pockets a lipstick, a compact, a jar of some kind of cream, a thing of gum that had five packages in it, and a chocolate bar. "I never buy anything in the dime store."

I was stunned. "You stole them?"

"I took them. They don't care. They don't know the difference. Didn't you ever take anything from the dime store?"

"No. I'd be scared stiff. Don't they ever catch you?"

"Of course not. Hell. My mother wanted some thread. You go back and get it."

"I'll buy it. I won't steal it."

She shook her head in disgust. "You are a baby. I dare you to go." She looked at me defiantly.

We stood there on Lexington Avenue staring at each other. There was something both good and evil in Millie—she looked like one of her own caricatures.

We went back into the store and she took the thread, picking out the color she wanted like she was going to pay a fortune for it, and she slipped it into her hand and her pocket with me hardly seeing her do it. It was creepy.

"I thought your mother had left by now," I said. Her mother's film job had been postponed and every week Millie had said she was about to leave.

"She's leaving tomorrow," she said in a funny, sharp voice.

"Didn't you want to stay home with her to-day?" The minute the words were out I was sorry. I knew I shouldn't have asked her.

Her eyes were blazing. "She's spending the day with Ricky."

"Do you want to come home and have supper with me?"

She shook her head. I don't think she could speak for fear of crying. I wanted to die. After a while she said, "I have to go home and pack. I'm going over to live with the Rizzos."

"Are those the people you don't like?"

"They're not so bad. They're an Italian family. But they live in a crummy house and they have a bunch of little kids. I won't even have a room to myself, and they live over a bar that plays a jukebox all night long. It gets on my nerves."

I left her at the subway station. There was something terribly sad about seeing her disappear down the subway stairs in those crazy slacks and creepy jacket. I took a crosstown bus and ran all the way from the bus stop to my house. I wanted to get home.

I'd told Mom I'd gone to the museum with Millie, and Didi had to butt in. "You went with that creep! I don't know how you can stand her."

"Shut up."

"You shut up."

"I'll talk when I want to . . ."

"Stop it." Mom sounded irritated, and tired, too.

I went into my room and slammed the door and sat down to try to write here, but I couldn't. I played some records to calm down.

A lot of good it does to have an interesting afternoon. No one asks me a single question about it.

Something peculiar happened. Last night at the dinner table I made an announcement. "I hope no one tells me what to do spring vacation," I said. "I want to have time to myself. I want to sleep late—I'll make my own breakfast, Mom, don't worry—go out when I want, come home when I want—oh, not late at night, but eat when I want, read when I want. I don't want to live on a schedule."

"Who do you think you are?" Didi said. "You're living in a house with other people. You can't have everything your own way."

"You seem to do it most of the time. Besides, it's none of your business. I'm asking Mom, not you." Then I looked at Mom and I almost died. Her eyes were full of tears.

"I want free time too, Sarah. I'm not complaining, but I seem to always be running here, running there, and at the end of the day it's nothing but errands and chores . . ." Suddenly she burst into tears and left the table. Daddy, Didi, and I sat there stunned.

"You stupid idiot," yelled Didi. She got up to go after Mom. But my father was ahead of her. "Sit down, Didi. It's not Sarah's fault." His face was tense and white, and he strode out of the room after Mom.

Didi sat there glaring at me. "If Mom gets sick it's your fault," she said. "She has enough problems without your adding to them. Wanting free time. Hell, you don't do anything anyway. I think," she lowered her voice, "Mom is having a nervous breakdown."

"If she is it's because of you. You're the one who pushes her around, not me. You're always trying to wheedle something out of her."

"Be quiet and finish your supper."

"Don't tell me what to do."

Daddy came back in a while grimmer than before. "Your mother isn't feeling well. Hurry up with your supper, girls, and do the dishes." He went into the kitchen and made some coffee for himself and sat at the table drinking it. Nobody said anything until I couldn't stand it.

"She didn't get upset because of what I said, did she?" I had my eyes on Dad's solemn face.

"I doubt it. Maybe we've all been expecting too much of her. She gets tired like everyone else."

"She does an awful lot of running around.

She took Sarah's books back to the library and went all the way down to the Village to get a kooky wool hat Sarah wanted." Didi was still glaring at me.

"That's a lie. She said she was going to the library for herself and she was down in the Village anyway. She didn't go just for me."

"Will you two please shut up? The bickering that goes on between you is enough to wear anyone out. Your mother's tired, that's all. And I am too, so let's have some quiet."

After supper I went into my room but I left my door open. I wanted to know what was going on, and I wanted to see Mom if I could. I was worried about her. And I made a vow: I vowed that I wasn't going to let Didi bug me any more even when she picked on me. I was going to stay calm, and just be polite and nice to her.

March Still

Mom really is sick. The house is like a morgue, it's awful. She's terribly depressed and when I come home from school she's usually lying down. When she gets up it's almost worse because she goes around the house like a zombie, trying to be with it, but her mind is a million miles away. Last night she put a kettle on the stove and forgot all about it, and the whole pot almost burnt up. I don't know what to do because my saying I didn't want to be pushed around is what set her off. I feel scared. When I'm in school I forget about it for a little while, but when I come home it starts all over again.

Mrs. L. asked me about my play. I told her I hadn't thought of one yet, but in the meantime I have to write a short story. It's about a girl a little like Millie only older, who wants to be an artist but her family doesn't want her to be. They think artists are kooky. Anyway, she runs away from home and hides in the Metropolitan Museum. She lives on hot dogs and pretzels that she buys from the men outside with the carts, and she studies the paintings in the museum. At night she hides in some dark place where the guards can't see her. Anyway, she makes a painting that is terrific. It is so good the museum wants to buy it, and they decide not to punish her for hiding there, and her family is very proud of her. She goes home and becomes a famous painter.

Later

Didi is obnoxious. I hate her. I asked her if she thought I had made Mom sick, and she looked me straight in the eye and said yes. She *knew* I was looking for reassurance, that I'm really worried, and she knows what she said was a lie.

I got so mad I slapped her in the face. I really did. I don't know where I got the nerve. She was flabbergasted. Her face turned white and she grabbed hold of both my wrists and twisted them until I nearly screamed but I didn't utter a sound. "Don't you dare ever do a thing like that again," she said. "Don't you dare. Get out of my room and don't come in it again." I picked Midnight up from the floor and left.

All afternoon and all through supper she was silent, and I could feel the hate pouring out of her. If she wasn't so mean I'd feel sorry for her. I think something's going on between her and Ronnie. I heard her ask Ellen on the phone if

Ronnie was going over to Ellen's to help her with her math. I don't think she likes that very much. Ellen is supposed to be her best friend, but I think Didi's jealous of her. Ellen can stay out as late as she pleases and that bugs Didi, especially when Ellen and her date and Ronnie have to bring Didi home first. I wouldn't trust Ellen for a minute.

March

So much is happening. Mom is going to a psychiatrist. Dad seems nervous about it although he says he is glad and that he hopes Mom will get help.

Grandma picked me up at school this afternoon and we went for a walk. She is fantastic. I love her. She comes right out with everything without any fuss, and she doesn't talk to me as if I were a baby or an idiot.

"I want to talk to you about your mother," she said. "She's my daughter, and I love her as much as you do, even though we haven't always gotten along perfectly.

74

"Your mother is going through a hard time. I think it's partly a pre-menopause upset. A lot of women go through it, but I think Elsa is having it a little rougher than others. Part of it, I think, is because she gave up her music, her career, and now you girls are growing up and she's worried about the future. What she's going to do when you two leave home. Do you know what menopause is?"

"I'm not sure." I was trying not to be scared, but I was.

"You haven't started your period yet, have you? Well, it's when a woman goes into the next part of her life, when her period stops. The body goes through a lot of changes, and some women get depressed. It's not serious and these days a doctor can give you pills if you need them. Your mother will be fine, but you and Didi have to be very patient with her now. And not make demands."

"I try not to. I don't know about Didi."

"In some ways you're more independent than Didi."

"Do you really think so?" I was amazed. "But Didi always knows what she wants and I don't."

"Didi's older and should know what she wants

more than you do. You don't have to make any important choices yet."

"I hope I'm somebody when I grow up."

"If you want to be you will be. I'm not worried about you."

I felt good until I came home. Mom came home from her doctor looking like a ghost and I think she was sick in the bathroom. I hope I don't have to go through the menopause like that. And she hasn't even got it yet, Grandma said it was *pre*-menopause.

Maybe Mom wished that she didn't have any children and that she could travel and still be a concert pianist. I think she could anyway. I wouldn't mind living here with Daddy and maybe Grandma would live with us. But there'd still be Didi. Maybe Mom would go away and take Didi with her and Dad and I would be alone. I could take care of the house. I'd get rid of a lot of the stuff we have and just keep what we need.

But when I see how sad Mom looks I feel awful having such thoughts. When I'm with Mom I do love her. It's when I'm alone and she's with Didi that I think of her being far away.

April

Out of a clear sky Mutsie asked me, "Am I still your best friend?"

"Sure. Why do you ask?"

"I thought maybe Millie was your best friend." She had a funny look on her face.

"You can have two good friends, can't you?"

"I like to have one best friend," she said.

"Millie's been having a hard time, living with those people she doesn't like. Her mother's away on a job. I feel sorry for her."

"I don't. She's a creep." Mutsie looked at me intently with those button eyes of hers. "Millie has a dirty mind. She called Miss Stanley a lesbian because she puts her arm around the girls. I think maybe Millie is queer. She acts as if she were your boyfriend. She's jealous of everyone else you see. She's jealous every time you and I have a date. I know it."

"You're nuts. Millie isn't jealous of anyone. She likes to be alone. I'm not even sure if she likes me or not."

"She does. In a creepy way. You'd better be careful."

"You're crazy," I said. But what Mutsie said

gave me the shivers. Next time we had gym I watched Miss Stanley like crazy, and every time she did put her arm around a girl, Mutsie sent me those looks of hers until I nearly died. But I don't believe it. I wish Mutsie hadn't said anything, now it's all I can think of when I look at Miss Stanley.

Wow. Mrs. L. likes my story. She said I had a lot of imagination. She wants me to re-write it with some of her suggestions. Maybe it will get printed in our school magazine that comes out the end of the year. That would be fantastic.

April, the next day

Didi really got hell last night. Even Mom got mad at her. Didi said that Millie had started a rumor in school that Miss S. was queer. Dad and Mom both jumped on her. "How do you know Millie started it?" Mom asked.

"If it was a rumor you have no business repeating it," Dad said.

"Everyone's repeating it," Didi said.

"That's no excuse. That makes it worse." Dad

was fuming. "Whatever Miss Stanley is, is her business."

Dad gave it to her the most and Mom was on his side.

They asked me if I had heard the same rumor and I had to admit I had. "But I don't believe it."

"You're a liar," Didi shrieked. "You and that friend of yours, Mutsie, have been spreading it all over school."

"That's an absolute lie," I said, trying not to shriek the way she did. "I haven't repeated it to a soul."

"Don't believe her," Didi screamed.

"Stop it." Dad was sharp. "I can't stand you two screaming at each other."

"I wasn't screaming," I said calmly.

"There will be no rumors in this house," my mother said. "The only way to scotch a rumor is not to repeat it. I don't want to hear any more about it."

Later Dad and Mom went for a walk, and I could hear Didi on the telephone with Ellen complaining about her family, especially me. But she hung up pretty abruptly and she looked miserable. I think Ellen must have told her

Ronnie was coming over again to help her with her homework. Ellen's either dumb or smart as a fox, I don't know which.

Then something awful happened. I borrowed one of Didi's records—a new good one. It's funny the way we can be screaming at each other one minute and then be kind of friends the next. Anyway, after I played the record I put it on my bed, and I forgot about it and sat on it. It broke.

I really felt terrible. I was scared stiff to go and tell her, although I made up my mind I'd save my money and buy her a new one.

But she didn't get mad at all. "It's only a record," she said. Her eyes were sad as if she was worried. I never know what to expect from her.

April

My life is peculiar. We all had to go to see Mom's shrink. Mom was pretty nervous. She changed her clothes about three times and kept asking Didi and me what we were going to wear. As if we were going to a party or something. Dad had to leave his studio to meet us there.

His office is on Fifth Avenue so we all got into a taxi. I'd never been to a psychiatrist's office before. The waiting room was posh with a big soft rug and pictures. Mommy laughed and said that psychiatrists were rich as hell. When she told me she paid him forty dollars a visit I nearly fainted.

The shrink is young (I thought he'd be an old man) with glasses and not bad looking. Didi started batting her eyes at him right away. If he's fooled by Didi he's a simp. We all sat around for a few minutes not saying anything—it was awful. He asked Mom how she was feeling, and she told him she was nervous. So he asked her why, and that started things off. Mom said she felt guilty spending all that money going to a psychiatrist, and Dad said that was nonsense, the important thing was for her to be well, and Didi said the same thing. He asked me how I felt about it and I said of course I wanted Mom to be well but I didn't see why it had to cost so much money to sit and talk to him. He must have thought that was funny because he actually laughed.

Mom, Dad, and Dr. Miller did most of the talking. The whole thing was fantastic. At one point Mom got emotional and said that she loved us and she felt that she was failing us—that she hated putting us through all this, being depressed, that she wanted to be cheerful and someone we could count on. That got me weepy and like an idiot I bawled.

Of course he asked me why I was crying and I mumbled that I loved Mom the way she was, that I didn't have to count on her, I just wanted to feel close.

"Don't you feel close?"

"Not always."

"Why not?"

Then I said it. "I think she's closer to Didi." That stinker creep of a doctor. I wish he hadn't made me say it. Mom got upset and said it wasn't true. That bastard doctor just sat there not saying a word, letting us cry and all talk at each other until he said, "That's enough for today, our time is up. I think it will be useful if we all get together again soon," he added with his blank face. Mom walked out with her arm around me and I felt awful for what I said.

Surprise. Mom was waiting for me when I came out of school yesterday. She looked prettier than she has for a long while. She'd been going around in sacky old clothes, but yesterday she had on her good slacks and sweater.

"Let's go for a walk," she said. I knew she had something on her mind. I could tell by her face.

We walked down Central Park West but I persuaded her to come into the park and we sat down on a bench.

She said she was sorry about getting upset and upsetting me, and she wanted me to know that she loved me as much as she did Didi. "Maybe I show it in different ways," she said, "because Didi is older and has problems that we talk about. When you're older you may want to confide in me or maybe not. I think you live more within yourself than Didi does and your relationships with people will be different from hers. You and Didi are very different."

"I don't know what I am," I said.

"Of course not, not yet. You're still developing into your own person, with your own point of view. That's what counts. Your ideals are high and sometimes they get in your way, but that's all right. You expect people to be perfect and they're not. Didi has plenty of faults and you get outraged by them, why? You have to accept her as she is."

"I can't stand it when she acts high-hat and phony."

"You don't have to. That's her problem, not yours. It's foolish to let yourself get so irritated. You probably have mannerisms that drive her up the wall too. After all, you're not going to live with Didi all your life."

"But I'm living with her now. She can be such a pain."

"You're intolerant, Sarah. You never look at Didi's good qualities."

"Has she any?" I asked gloomily.

Mom laughed. "Didi loves you very much. She gets concerned about you. Did it ever occur to you that she might be jealous of you? After all, she was kingpin before you came along. Having a bright kid sister like you is something to cope with."

"Didi thinks I'm a creep. She wishes I was dead."

Mom looked at me sharply. "Maybe you wish that of her."

I didn't answer. We got nowhere. It was a dead-end conversation. We walked home and Mom looked less perky than when we started. I felt sad all over again. It was a glorious day and I wished we hadn't discussed problems.

We passed Howard on the way home and he gave us a big hello. Mom said she liked him because he was so outgoing. I think Mom enjoys Didi having a boyfriend even if she complains Didi sees too much of him. Maybe she just says it because she thinks she has to. She's going to be very disappointed in me because I'm not going to have a "boyfriend" for years and years.

April Sunday

Yesterday was a nice day. I like Saturdays, I can stay in bed late, and I usually wash my hair and hang around in my bathrobe being lazy. The phone rang early and for a change it wasn't for Didi. It was Howard for me. He said he had to write a composition about something in New

85

York, and he was thinking of going up to Ft. Tryon Park to the Cloisters and did I want to go with him. It sounded super. He said his mother would make a picnic lunch for the two of us.

Mom and Didi got all excited. I told them to cool it. It was only Howard and we were only going up to the park for his homework. But Mom came in to pick out what I should wear and Didi insisted on brushing my hair. Like they were really cuckoo.

Dad asked what all the fuss was about, and I told him, "Nothing. I'm going up to the Cloisters with Howard. I don't know what these two are making a fuss about."

Dad bawled out Mom and Didi. "I can't believe you," he said. "She's only a child. You're carrying on like she was eighteen." Mom and Didi only giggled and teased him and said that he didn't like to see his girls growing up. They embarrassed me. I was glad when Howard appeared with his bag of lunch.

We went over to Riverside Drive and took a bus uptown. Howard is outgoing and easy to be with. He told me about his uncle who's a pilot and flies to England and France and sometimes to Africa. Someday he's going to take Howard to Africa. Howard's not sure if he wants to be a pilot, or maybe a game warden in Africa. He'd like to save wildlife from getting destroyed.

The Cloisters is a terrific place. We were both starving when we got there so we ate our lunch outside. The statues are beautiful, I like them better than the paintings, and the tapestries are fabulous. It's hard to believe that people made every stitch in those tapestries by hand. Every stone of the Cloisters was brought over from Spain, and Howard and I thought about monks or nuns (we didn't know which) having walked along paths just like those and through the colonnades. I like Howard because he's not silly. He's very serious and he knows a lot. He can also be funny.

After we left the park we walked along the drive and then climbed down so we could be near the river. A man came along in a motorboat and waved to us and signaled, asking if we wanted a ride, but we said no. Howard and I made up stories about his being a kidnapper or running illegal drugs or maybe he had just murdered someone and needed an alibi. Probably he was just lonesome.

Everyone was ready to sit down to supper when I got home. Dad was mad that I'd come home so late, but Mom and Didi wanted to know what we did. I told them we'd had our lunch and walked around. Mom wanted to know what we had for lunch. They were both asking me to tell about my day.

"She's not talking," Didi said, and she and Mom exchanged glances.

"There's nothing to talk about," I told them.

"She's got more sense than you have," Dad said glancing at the two of them.

I felt peculiar.

May

I can't believe the way time goes. Almost the end of school, almost time to go to Truro.

It is so springy out, I love it. We went on a real family picnic. It was Mom's idea and Dad was very pleased that Mom wanted to do something, she's been so out of it. Even Didi agreed to come, which made it like old times.

Mom made a fantastic lunch, fried chicken

and tomatoes and brownies and we took a bottle of wine. We drove up to Croton-on-Hudson. Mom wanted to find a quarry where she used to swim when she was a girl. We drove around looking for it but we never did find it. Mom said it probably had a development on it now, but she was disappointed, although she pretended it was okay.

We found a quiet, shady piece of woods to picnic in and then we sat around after we ate. Dad was reading the Sunday paper and Mom was almost asleep. But Didi kept looking at her watch.

"Do you want to go for a walk?" I asked her.

She shook her head. "No. I'd really like to go home."

"But it's only the middle of the afternoon."

"I know. I shouldn't have come. I want to be home by five or five-thirty the latest."

"Daddy said maybe we'd have supper out."

"You three can, I want to go home." She looked worried.

I felt myself getting mad at her. "One of your dumb dates."

"I've got to see Ronnie tonight. It's really important."

"You'll see him in school tomorrow." I couldn't believe why she was getting emotional.

"You don't understand. I've got to see him tonight." She was so intense it was scary.

"Well, tell Dad," I said.

"He'll bawl me out," said Didi.

"You want me to tell him?"

"Will you?" I was so surprised. It was like a shock to have her ask me something like that. I couldn't be mad at her any more for breaking up our picnic. I really wanted to help her.

"Didi wants to go home," I told Dad.

She was right. He got mad. Said she had no business making a date when she knew we were going away for the day, that it wouldn't hurt her to spend a day with her family, that she knew it meant a lot to Mom, and to him and to me, Sarah.

Then I piped up. "I don't care if she wants to go home. I've got homework to do anyway," I lied. I didn't really. Didi looked at me like she was real grateful.

"If the girls want to leave, let's go," Mom said. "It's been a lovely day and maybe we've had enough."

Dad still grumbled, but we left.

Didi actually came into my room before she went out to meet Ronnie and said, "Thanks for helping me out."

"That's okay," I told her, but I felt fantastic.

May

I think I must be backward. Both Mutsie and Charlotte got their period and I haven't. Now they both act as if they had grown up and I haven't, which is stupid. But what if I don't get it? I can't ask Mom if there are some girls who never do because I'm not supposed to upset her about anything now. And I'd feel too dumb asking Didi. I hope Mom hurries up and gets well. Now she has a thing about elevators and subways; she won't go near the subway and gets all tense every time we go up and down in the elevator.

The most fantastic thing has happened. MY STORY IS GOING TO BE IN *The Ink Pot,* our school magazine. I can't believe it. Mrs. L. told me today. She's the faculty adviser, the rest of the board are juniors and seniors. It made me feel better than a million birthdays and Christmases. Even that drip Mr. Harris congratulated me. Didi did too. Mom and Dad hugged me and said they were very proud. I don't think anyone knows how great it makes me feel. I don't think I will ever get depressed again. I can't wait to see it in print. Mrs. L. seemed almost as excited as I am.

I'd die if I didn't have this diary to put everything down in, because there's no one to talk to.

Dad told Didi and me that he wanted to take Mom to the country on Saturday and come back Sunday. "I want to be alone with her. Do you think I can trust you two girls here alone overnight? Grandma's away visiting a friend in Virginia for a week."

We both said, "Of course." And that he shouldn't worry. For once Didi didn't make a fuss about taking care of me.

I should have guessed something was up. Mom and Dad both gave us a bunch of instructions about how we shouldn't open the door to anyone, and that Didi had to stay home Saturday night, and what there was for us to eat, etc., etc. It was a relief when they left. I spent Saturday afternoon with Mutsie and came home around six o'clock.

Didi was in her room but the door was open. I knew the minute I saw her she'd been crying.

"What's the matter?" I asked.

She gave me one look and started crying again. "Ronnie and I've split up . . . he's going with Ellen . . . he's taking her out tonight . . ." I was flabbergasted.

"That lousy rat," I said.

"It's Ellen . . . she did it. If we'd just split up it wouldn't be so bad, but to think that she'd do such a thing. . . . I'll have to see them in school every day. I can't stand it . . . I thought she was my friend and she knew how I felt about Ronnie . . ."

"It's the lousiest thing I ever heard of." I wished I knew how to comfort her. What to say . . .

"I'm never going to trust anyone again as long as I live."

"You can trust me," I said.

She almost smiled. "I have to trust you now." Then she stopped crying and looked at me very earnestly. "I don't want Mom or Dad to know."

"But they'll know that you've stopped seeing them."

"They may not notice and they don't have to know why. I can just say they're busy with exams or something. We will be, anyway."

"I won't tell. I promise."

"I feel so awful. They're probably both laughing at me . . ." She started crying again.

"To hell with them. They're not worth it. Maybe you should switch to another school." Having to see them in school would be horrible.

"I can't, not when I'm going into my senior year. Sarah, tell me the truth. Do you think there's something wrong with me? Why would anyone do this to me?"

"Don't be cuckoo. You're terrific. There's something wrong with them, not you." I couldn't believe my own ears.

I do really think she was glad she told me, and that I made her feel better. I finally got her into the kitchen and we fixed dinner and she was even able to joke a little. "I've been jilted," she said. "I never thought it could happen to me. I saw it coming and I should have split up with him first. But I didn't want to believe that Ronnie going over to Ellen to help her with her math meant anything. I was an ass, I thought he was being nice because Ellen was my friend. Don't ever fall in love, Sarah."

"I have no intention to," I told her. We watched some dopey television and ate potato chips, and I think she felt better by the time we went to bed.

But I am in a real turmoil. I honestly feel bad that this happened to Didi, but at the same time I feel good because she told me. It made me feel close to her and like a real sister. But why did it have to happen because she was unhappy?

Still May

And still confused about Didi. She goes around looking awful and Mom thinks she's worried about exams. It's pretty fantastic how parents and kids live in the same house and see each other every day, and they don't know what goes on with each other. I'm trying hard to be nice to Didi, playing my records very low and not hogging the bathroom.

May

Didi is desperate. "I've got to get away this summer," she said to me.

"Where do you want to go?"

"Europe. I know about a group that's going."

I was astonished. "Because of Ronnie and Ellen?" I asked.

"Yes. I can't stand it. I keep thinking about them being together all the time."

"What will Mom and Dad say?"

"I don't know . . ." She looked so pale. I wanted to put my arm around her but she was so distant.

Mom and Dad had nothing but objections. "I suppose it's because Ronnie and Ellen are going?" Mom asked.

"They have nothing to do with it. They're not part of the group." I didn't dare look at her.

"How come you're so anxious to go away?" Dad asked.

"It's going to be a fabulous trip," said Didi.

"We can't afford it," Dad said.

"It's not that expensive. We go on a student rate."

"I was looking forward to having you at home," Mom said. "This may be your last summer to spend with your family. Sarah will be all alone."

"I don't mind," I said. "This may be her last chance to go to Europe this way. You said that when she goes to college she'll have to work in the summer."

Mom and Dad were surprised. "You're the one who always objects to Didi breaking up the family," Mom said. "This is a switch."

"It's only for three weeks, it's not the whole summer," I argued.

It was a switch, me rooting for Didi. Even though Didi and I can hardly ever say thank you to each other, I knew she appreciated it. It was like the currents in our family were shifting. Nothing was decided that night but I felt good speaking up for Didi instead of against her.

I had a conference with Mrs. L.

"I'm so pleased about your story. But what about the play you wanted to write?" she asked. "Are you still thinking about it?"

"Yes I am. I think I'll write it over the summer."

"That will be fine. But don't you want to be outdoors in the summer?"

"Some of the time. But I think I can do it."

"It will take a lot of self-discipline, Sarah."

"But I really like to write, honestly I do."

"Mr. Harris thinks that getting your story published in *The Ink Pot* has gone to your head."

"Mr. Harris doesn't know anything about my head," I said, "or anything else for that matter," I mumbled.

Mrs. L. gave me a funny look, but she didn't disagree. She's okay.

June
_____

It's going to be a fantastic summer. I can hardly

stand thinking about it. I get scared when everything seems great—I think something awful will happen to spoil it. I play dopey games like thinking if the next car that comes along is red that's a good sign. I kind of keep my eyes half closed waiting for the first red car. It's cheating but I have to make it come out right.

It's all settled. Didi is going to Europe. Mom is still worrying about my being alone, and what will I do with myself, blah-blah-blah. But I'm looking forward to being alone. Isn't it weird? You think when you feel something, like when I hated Didi to go off without me, it's going to be forever. And then all of a sudden everything changes. I'm glad she's going and I wish it were for longer than three weeks. Actually I think she will be away from me longer because she's going to spend a week or two in New York with Mom getting ready and I'll be up at the Cape with Grandma. That will be super.

June

WE'RE HERE. In our salty-smell, wonderful

house in Truro. I love it. When I'm a little old lady I'm going to live here all the time with a dog and a boat and wear a big sunbonnet and turn up my nose at all the tourists. We've had this house since I was four years old and I get excited the minute we cross the bridge over the canal and are truly on the Cape. It smells different from any place, and it *is* different.

Our house sits up high on top of the dunes and I can look down and see the bay, my breakwater with its flat rocks where I love to sit, and the cove where Dad lets me take the Sailfish by myself. I can also see the curve of Provincetown with its twinkly lights at night. I like it best early in the morning when the tide is out and I can walk way out on the sandbars that don't have a footprint on them except from the sandpipers and then the ones that I make. I feel special then. I even feel I'm beautiful.

June

My life is sure full of surprises. But maybe things do change.

100

Dad, Mom, Didi, and I were sitting out on the deck. Mom and Dad were having drinks when Dad asked if we had any projects for the summer. Didi said she was going to spend time reading up on the places she'd be seeing in Europe.

Then Dad asked how I intended to use my time this summer. I calmly announced I was going to write a play.

Holy cow! You'd think I'd said I was going to murder my grandmother, the way it hit Dad. "What do you know about writing a play? You've hardly been to the theatre, and it's probably the most difficult form of writing there is. You've done a good short story, why don't you stick to that? People struggle for years to write a play . . . Blah, blah, blah."

"There's no harm in her trying," Mom said gently.

"She should have respect for a craft. With all due respect for *The Ink Pot*, she still has lots to learn about writing a short story, and I think she should try to master one form before she starts on another."

"But I want to write a play." I was stunned by Dad's reaction.

"Why don't you leave her alone?" Didi spoke up. "If she wants to write a play the least you can do is encourage her. I don't believe you, Dad—the only way to learn is by doing it. What's got into you?"

"I was just expressing my opinion," Dad said looking hurt. "Everyone doesn't have to jump on me."

"But you were jumping on Sarah," Didi said.

End of conversation about my play. But can you believe Didi, speaking up for me?

Sunday night — June

We just came home from driving Dad to the airport to take his plane back to New York after the weekend. This afternoon Dad and I had a long walk on the beach and we talked about what he said about my play. He said that he was sorry if he had been too negative, but that because he was an artist he had a tremendous respect for craft and art forms. That everyone thinks that they can write or paint, but only the true artist knows that creative work doesn't come easily—that it takes a lot of work to master techniques before you can create freely. It was a good, serious discussion, and I was glad we had it. He doesn't treat me like an idiot.

June

I spent the afternoon down at the breakwater. There and in the little cove. It's where the Pamet River comes into the bay, and you can sit inside one of the dunes and look up at the sky and watch the clouds. No one can see you. Part of the time I stretched out on the rocks and looked down between the crevices to watch the fish and the crabs. I gathered some beautiful shells and thought about what Dad had said and about my play. I can't see anything so mysterious about a play, and I'm going to try. I want to write about sisters, and I keep thinking about Cinderella. I wonder if I could write a modern Cinderella—someone who didn't think going to a ball was the greatest thing in the world?

I have decided I will write a Cinderella play. I might be criticized for copying something but I think for a first play that is not too bad. Especially after what Dad said. I am excited about it. I'd have the two stinky sisters and Cindy, the drudge. The first scene the two lazy sisters would sit around playing records and drinking soda and eating popcorn while Cindy did all the work. They would be pretty mean talking about the big ball they were going to, and putting on all their slinky, sexy dresses (which would be far from becoming), trying to decide what to wear. They would talk about their clothes and boyfriends, and they'd ask Cindy to clean their shoes and sew on buttons, and wash and press their clothes.

But I have to figure out why Cindy would do it. She'd have to be pretty sappy to hang around waiting on them. She could have no money and no place to go—they could live in an imaginary kingdom, and their house could be in some out of the way place that is hard to get out of. And there would be no jobs for women.

I'm going to write some dialogue and then go swimming.

July

The minute everything seems settled and smooth, it all gets mixed up again. Didi is in a state. She packs and unpacks and keeps remembering something else she has to buy. "They have toothpaste and panty hose and talcum powder in England and France," I said.

"Yes, I know," she said. But her mind was far away.

"Are you excited?"

She looked at me as if she hadn't realized I was there. "I'm scared."

"You scared?" It was a shock—the last thing I would ever imagine. "But you'll be with a whole group. You won't be alone."

She nodded. "I know, but I don't know any of them well. Damn," she said viciously. "If it wasn't for Ellen and Ronnie I wouldn't be going on this trip. Ronnie and I had talked about his coming up here for a few weeks, before . . ." Her eyes watered.

"Forget about them." Holy cow, I felt like her big sister.

"I wish I could."

"That's why you're going away. You'll have a fantastic time, you'll see."

"I doubt it . . . but I hope so." She looked miserable.

I felt peculiar telling her I was going to spend the day with Howard who was in Wellfleet for a week or so with his parents. But I'm just friends with Howard so I guess that's different.

Mom drove Howard and me and our bikes to P-town and left us at the beginning of the bike trail near Race Point. The trail was empty except for us and we rode way out along the dunes and marshland where we stopped and watched the birds. I like Howard because he doesn't talk about nature but you know he feels it. He doesn't keep saying this or that is beautiful, but you can tell by his silence that he feels it inside the way I do. And he knows the names of all the birds, too.

I told Howard a little bit about my play and he asked me how I was going to end it.

"I haven't got that far yet," I said.

"Cindy could murder her two sisters," he suggested.

"Then she'd have to go to jail. I wouldn't like that."

"She doesn't have to get caught."

"But she'd worry about it the rest of her life."

"What do you care? You can end the play with a double murder."

He was very pleased, but his idea was awful. He did not understand that while Cindy is some-one I made up (or borrowed from Cinderella) she was a real person to me. I don't think I'd like her to commit a double murder even if she didn't get caught.

When we came back from the trail we rode into P-town and sat on the wharf watching the fishing boats come in. We bought hot dogs and jelly apples and had a good time eating them.

July

Writing a play is very hard. I get worried that some of the advice Dad gave me may be true. Everything has to happen with people talking, and on a stage they cannot rush off to different places. I cannot have a lot of sets because that is very expensive. And I haven't told anyone, but Mrs. L. said that if my play was good, *maybe* our class could put it on at school. Wouldn't that be fantastic?

The first scene is written, and it is pretty good. The sisters push Cindy around until a person wants to scream at her to punch them. But she is too timid to hit anybody. The sisters go off and Cindy is alone on stage; she dreams out loud of a prince coming to rescue her and her sisters doing all the work while she is queen. Of course she never expects such a thing to happen, and she continues to mop the floor.

I think in the next scene she will meet the fairy godmother, except in my play the fairy godmother will be more like a guru, Oriental and dressed in long robes. I have it all in my head, but when I write it down on paper it doesn't come out exactly the same.

Millie is coming up to visit me and I think maybe I will let her read it. After all she showed me her drawings so I think it would be only fair for me to reciprocate.

Didi gets more and more nervous as the time draws near for her leaving. I am glad I am not in love because I would hate having anything so foolish interfere with my going to Europe. It is amazing that I was ever jealous of Didi when I now see that all her laughing and her acting and pointed opinions and being a good athlete do not help her get out of a rut. I would not waste a thought on rats like Ellen and Ronnie.

Howard is going home tomorrow and Didi made remarks about my "boyfriend" which I ignored.

Howard and I went to the beach at Longnook and walked for miles and miles. He likes boats and now he thinks he might want to design ships when he grows up but he is worried that there may not be ships any more because people like to get places in a hurry so they go by plane. I hope for his sake that some people will still want to go on ships.

On our way back the clouds got dark and the ocean rough, like it could be the end of the world. I thought walking into the dark, whirling mass of ocean and wind might be a nice way to die. However, since we both wanted to go home instead of dying, we ran. A tremendous crack of thunder and a great flash of lightning made us run very fast. I pretended I wasn't afraid, and it is quite possible that Howard was doing the same. It was pouring by the time we got to our bikes, and we had a wild, crazy ride to Route #6 where we ran into a hamburger place. We only had enough money for one hot dog which we divided evenly.

I like Howard very much, but contrary to Mom's and Didi's remarks I will not feel lonesome when he goes home. It is a bit of a strain being with a boy because you cannot say the same things to him that you would to a girl friend like Millie or Mutsie. It must be very trying to live with someone of the opposite sex when you are not used to it. If I had to see Howard in the morning when I got up, and all day long, I could never do anything normal like have a stomachache or go to the bathroom or pick my nose.

Didi has left. I must say it was a big relief when she and Mom and Dad drove off to Kennedy Airport. Didi looked very nice in a new pants suit and I thought how funny that she was going to be on the other side of the ocean that I went swimming in every day. I gave her a big bar of chocolate because she says that eating chocolate calms her nerves, and a very good paperback mystery. She made too much of a fuss about them, but I think she liked them in spite of her exaggerated thanks.

Grandma was as relieved as I was. "You'd think she was going to Europe," Grandma said, and we both thought that was a very good joke.

Grandma makes me feel good. We giggle one minute and get into a serious conversation the next. We get up early in the morning and walk out on the sandbar and then come back and make breakfast; not ordinary bacon and eggs and cereal but fresh fish we buy at the wharf, and pie and cheese. One morning she made pancakes. After breakfast we work. I work on my play and Grandma writes letters or does laundry or shops. We take a picnic lunch and go somewhere—to one of the trails or to a beach or a pond. When we come home we have supper. Grandma is a fantastic cook. One night we had lobster.

August

Grandma's gone and Mom came back with Millie. At first I was a little sorry because I was having a good time alone with Grandma, but I think it's going to be okay. I don't miss Didi.

"Are you going to let me read your play?" Millie asked. I wish she had waited until I offered it. It made me nervous to watch her read it. She made so many faces I couldn't figure out what she was thinking. Writing a play is very hard. There are so many decisions to make.

Millie thought it was pretty good but we got into a big argument about how to end it. I've gotten as far as the guru giving Cindy her wish —a slinky dress and sports car to go to the ball in. Cindy thinks it's going to be fabulous, she goes to the ball with her mask on, but it's a terrible drag. She's bored stiff. Except for the prince who she has fun with. But the others are squares and bores, and the whole thing is stupid as far as she is concerned. Just the kind of thing her sisters would think was super. She loses her slipper at the ball, the prince comes and finds her. He wants her to be his wife and to come and live in the palace with him.

It's kind of mixed up between modern and old fashioned, but I think that's all right. It's when she goes back to the palace with the prince that I'm in trouble. The palace stinks, of course. Who wants to live in a palace with a bunch of dumb ladies-in-waiting, having to attend a lot of boring ceremonies and dress up all the time, besides needing to be careful of everything you say and do. As far as Cindy is concerned the whole thing is obnoxious. But then what?

Millie (who is getting more political all the time) thinks Cindy should find the whole world terrible and do something dramatic like commit suicide. She and Howard really want someone killed. Millie gave me a speech saying that the play would then be "a protest against a material-istic concept of life and against phony material values."

But I can't see what Cindy would accomplish

by committing suicide. Millie had no answer to that. I don't know what to do. I never realized that writing was such a responsibility.

August

Time is going by too fast. Didi's been gone two weeks and before I know it she'll be back.

I hadn't been thinking about her very much, but a funny thing happened. Millie and I were in P-town, and who should we see but Ronnie and Ellen. Half our school comes up to the Cape in the summer. There they were walking down the street holding hands, and they did look happy together. I didn't want to see them, but they saw us. They were very friendly, bought Millie and me ice-cream cones, and they acted like they were having a great time. It was creepy, because I'd been thinking of them both as horrors and there they were just ordinary people enjoying themselves. Ellen looked pretty.

When we left them Millie said, "Wasn't Ronnie your sister's boyfriend?"

I told her yes, but I didn't say anything more.

114

Then I got to feeling sorry for Didi. There she was maybe with a bunch of drips in Europe and she could have been here with Ronnie instead of Ellen, having a good time in P—town. It seemed unfair. I vowed to be especially nice to Didi when she came home.

Still August

Millie's gone home and it's nice to be alone— it'll only be for a short time because Didi will be home soon.

I think I know how to end my play. Millie did put some ideas into my head. I like the idea of Cindy not falling for all the gold and precious jewels and stuff in the palace, and thinking it's unfair for it all to be stored in one prince's vault. But heck, she doesn't have to kill herself because of it. I decided she should talk the prince, who's a good guy, into leaving the palace, dividing up all the riches among the people, and to go and live with her in her little cottage. The palace could be turned over to the people for a vacation resort. The sisters would have to go to work like everyone else, and it ends up with no one being very rich and no one being poor, and Cindy and the prince living happily ever after in their cottage.

It's a real neat feeling to have that solved. I can't wait to get it all written down. I don't want to stop to do anything—not even eat or go to the bathroom.

End of August

I finished my play. I can't believe it. It's like the greatest relief and excitement both. But I get nervous thinking of giving it to Mrs. L. If she doesn't like it maybe I'll be the one to end up killing myself.

We're going back to New York. Didi comes home in two days. Mom is busy closing up the house. I hate leaving it. Took my last walk on the sandbar.

September. Back in New York.

It happened. I got my period. Just like that. I must say that when I first saw the blood I got scared. But when I realized what it was, I ran to tell Mom and I felt terrific and excited. I guess I'm a woman now. It does make me feel different —like I've gone over to the other side. But I'm still me, Sarah Grinnell. Sex female, height five feet, weight 105 pounds, dark hair, hazel eyes, olive complexion. Me, a person who wrote a play.

September

Didi is home, and higher than a kite.

"I had a great time. Absolutely fantastic. We hardly slept at all . . . I have a bunch of pictures to show you . . . we saw everything. And the food was out of this world. I met a terrific girl and her brother . . . they live in Virginia and invited me to come spend Christmas with them. Can I go, Mom? I said yes, I was sure you'd let me . . ."

I didn't think she'd ever stop talking. I felt funny thinking of Ronnie and Ellen up in P-town, and I wondered who had had the better summer, they or Didi—not that it mattered of course. I had told her to forget them, so why were they on my mind?

September—back in school

I did it. I gave Mrs. L. my play to read and I'm so nervous. I keep eating and going to the bathroom out of nervousness. Millie says I shouldn't care whether she likes it or not, but that's a lot of baloney.

September

I can't believe it. MY PLAY IS GOING TO BE PUT ON AT SCHOOL. Mrs. L. really likes it. She wants me to do some re-writing but I don't care. I can do it. Millie is going to design the set and maybe Mutsie will be Cindy.

I came home so excited. Mom and Dad are very proud. This is the most important thing that has ever happened to me.

Later

I still felt good so I said to Didi, "Do you want to read my play?"

"I'd love to, when I have time." We looked at each other and she laughed. "Maybe over the weekend, Sarah." She went into her room and here I am in mine.

I am going to be twelve years old in a few days and something extraordinary has happened. While Didi and I are sisters, I know now that we don't really connect. She has her life and I have mine. I don't think it has anything to do with her being a teen-ager and me being four years younger. We are simply different people. I guess I care about her, but not whether she reads my play or not. If she does, okay, if she doesn't, I won't care.

So long diary, I have to work on my play.